Trumpet

Alfred's
INSTRUMENTAL PLAY-ALONG

Top Praise & Worship
Instrumental Solos

MW00388031

CONTENTS

*Download free MP3 Demo and Play-Along tracks at www.alfred.com.
Simply enter product number 34234 into the search window to locate the book and corresponding recordings.*

Arranged by Bill Galliford, Ethan Neuburg and Tod Edmondson

© 2009 Alfred Music Publishing Co., Inc.
All Rights Reserved. Printed in USA.

Alfred

ISBN-10: 0-7390-6595-5
ISBN-13: 978-0-7390-6595-2

Track 2: Demo
Track 3: Play Along

EVERLASTING GOD

Words and Music by
BRENTON BROWN and KEN RILEY

Moderate rock (♩ = 112)

Verse:

Chorus:

Track 4: Demo
Track 5: Play Along

BEAUTIFUL ONE

Words and Music by
TIM HUGHES

5

Beautiful One - 2 - 2
34234

6

Track 6: Demo
Track 7: Play Along

BLESSED BE YOUR NAME

Words and Music by
BETH REDMAN and MATT REDMAN

Moderate rock (♩ = 120)   *Verse:*

GOD OF WONDERS

Track 8: Demo
Track 9: Play Along

Words and Music by
MARC BYRD and STEVE HINDALONG

THE WONDERFUL CROSS

Track 10: Demo
Track 11: Play Along

Words and Music by
CHRIS TOMLIN, J.D. WALT
and JESSE REEVES

HERE I AM TO WORSHIP
(LIGHT OF THE WORLD)

Track 12: Demo
Track 13: Play Along

Words and Music by
TIM HUGHES

YOU ARE MY ALL IN ALL

HOLY IS THE LORD

Words and Music by
CHRIS TOMLIN and LOUIE GIGLIO

Track 18: Demo
Track 19: Play Along

HOW GREAT IS OUR GOD

Words and Music by
CHRIS TOMLIN, ED CASH
and JESSE REEVES

Moderately slow rock (♩ = 76)

INDESCRIBABLE

Track 20: Demo
Track 21: Play Along

Words and Music by
JESSE REEVES and LAURA STORY

JESUS MESSIAH

Track 22: Demo
Track 23: Play Along

Words and Music by
DANIEL CARSON, CHRIS TOMLIN,
ED CASH and JESSE REEVES

Moderately slow (♩ = 84)

Verse 1:

20 Chorus:

36 Verse 2:

Jesus Messiah - 2 - 1
34234

LORD I LIFT YOUR NAME ON HIGH

Words and Music by
RICK FOUNDS

Lord I Lift Your Name on High - 2 - 1
34234

*Download free MP3 Demo and Play-Along tracks at www.alfred.com. Simply enter product number 34234 into the search window to locate the book and corresponding recordings.

Lord I Lift Your Name on High - 2 - 2
34234

MARVELOUS LIGHT

Words and Music by
CHARLIE HALL

*Download free MP3 Demo and Play-Along tracks at www.alfred.com. Simply enter product number 34234 into the search window to locate the book and corresponding recordings.

PARTS OF A TRUMPET AND FINGERING CHART

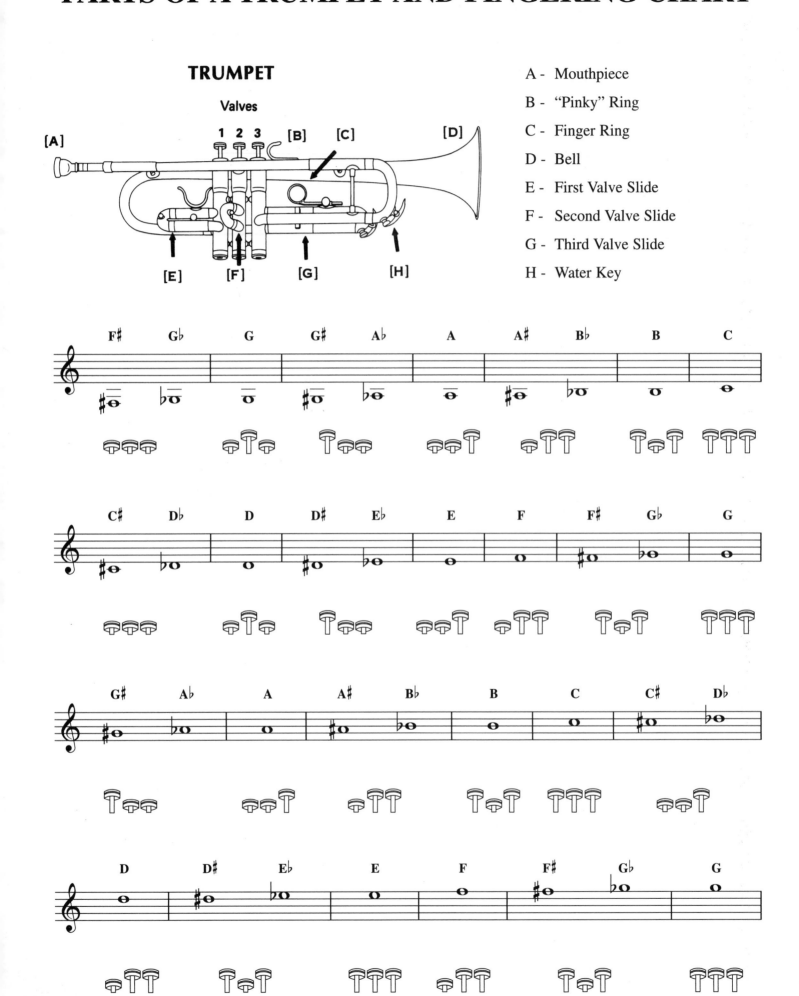